Also by Bruce Degen

I Said, "Bed!"

Snow Joke

by BRUCE DEGEN

Holiday House / New York

For Jan and Crosby,
the snowiest bunnies we know

I LIKE TO READ is a registered trademark of Holiday House, Inc.

Copyright © 2014 by Bruce Degen
All Rights Reserved
HOLIDAY HOUSE is registered in the U.S. Patent and Trademark Office.
Printed and Bound in April 2014 at Tien Wah Press, Johor Bahru, Johor, Malaysia.
The artwork was created with pen and ink, watercolor, colored pencil,
and gouache on 140 lb. Arches hot press paper.
www.holidayhouse.com
First Edition
1 3 5 7 9 10 8 6 4 2

Library of Congress Cataloging-in-Publication Data
Degen, Bruce, author, illustrator.
Snow joke / by Bruce Degen. — First edition.
pages cm. — (I like to read)
Summary: "After playing mean jokes on Bunny while they romp in the snow,
Red learns how to joke nicely"— Provided by publisher.
ISBN 978-0-8234-3065-9 (hardcover)
[1. Behavior—Fiction. 2. Jokes—Fiction. 3. Squirrels—Fiction.
4. Rabbits—Fiction.] I. Title.
PZ7.D3635Sno 2014
[E]—dc23
2013037253

Snow!

"Hey! Who threw that?"

"That's not funny," said Bunny.

"It's just a joke," said Red.
"Let's make a snowman."

"That's not funny," said Bunny.

"It's just a joke," said Red.

"Let's make snow angels."

"That's not funny," said Bunny.

"It's just a joke," said Red.

"Let's go sledding."

"That's not funny!"

"It's just a joke," said Red.

"Let's skate."

Red sped.

Red pushed.

Red fell.

"Waah!"

"That's a good joke," said Bunny.

"It's not funny!" said Red.

Everyone went to Bunny's house.

But where was Red?

Red was on the step.

"Have some cocoa," said Bunny.

Then Red told a
really good joke.
And everyone liked it.